Scuffy's Underground Adventure

By Mary Carey
Illustrated by Darrell Baker

A GOLDEN BOOK • NEW YORK
Western Publishing Company, Inc., Racine, Wisconsin 53404

Scuffy the tugboat had learned his lessons well. He had just returned from an early trip guiding a small cargo ship into the Little Golden Book Land harbor. Scuffy was smaller than the other tugboats in the harbor, and he had to work harder. But he knew he could do just as good a job.

"I may not be an ocean liner," he thought, "but I'm a good little craft all the same."

However, Scuffy was still young. Sometimes when the bigger tugboats were away, Scuffy got scared and lonely. He didn't like being all by himself when the sky grew dark at night.

As Scuffy was returning to the dock, he saw
Tootle on shore. Scuffy's friends Tawny Scrawny
Lion, Saggy Baggy Elephant, Shy Little Kitten, Poky
Little Puppy, and Baby Brown Bear were all there,
too, waiting on board the train.

"Scuffy, can you help us?" cried Tootle as Scuffy neared them.

"There is such trouble in Homeway Hollow," said Shy Little Kitten.

"Our well is running dry!" said Poky Little Puppy.

"Every day the water gets lower," explained Tootle. "Soon I'll have to haul water from the river."

"That means Tootle won't be able to help everybody get around Little Golden Book Land," said Baby Brown Bear.

"And that means we'll hardly ever get to see each other anymore," added Poky Little Puppy.

"Saggy Baggy Elephant tried to help, but he's so big he got stuck," said Baby Brown Bear.

"You're small," said Tawny Scrawny Lion. "You'd be able to fit in the well and find out what's happening to the water."

"But . . . but it's dark down in the well!" cried Scuffy before he knew what he was saying.

"You're right," agreed Tootle. "Maybe you're still too little to go down there by yourself. Thanks anyway, Scuffy. We'll try to think of someone else."

"I'm not too little," objected Scuffy. "And I'm not afraid of the dark. I'll put on my special night light and then I can do it."

So Saggy Baggy Elephant placed Scuffy in the special cargo car filled with water, and they all rumbled back to the town square in Homeway Hollow.

Tawny Scrawny Lion took Scuffy's towrope and slowly lowered him into the well.

Scuffy put on his light to see where he was. The walls were very close, and there was only a little water left down in the well. Had Scuffy been bigger, he would have scraped his keel on the bottom.

"But I'm not bigger," thought Scuffy, "I'm just the right size for this job."

Scuffy blew a brave blast on his whistle and set out to explore the underground streams that led into the well.

As Scuffy traveled on, the water got darker and darker, and Scuffy knew that he was very far underground. There was nothing shiny or bright about this water, and it felt very cold against his sides.

Scuffy shivered. "I'm not afraid of the dark. I'm not afraid of the dark," he told himself as he steamed on through the blackness.

And then, up ahead, Scuffy saw a sudden flash of movement. He took a deep breath and headed toward it. Something scurried along the wall beside the underground stream.

Scuffy jumped, and so did the scurrying creature.

"Who are you?" it asked.

"I . . . I . . . I'm Scuffy. Wh-who are you?" he said, trembling.

"Why, I'm a mole, of course, and I'm in the middle of my daily dig. I've been busy burrowing away for hours now. That's what we do, you know—moles, that is. We dig holes," said the mole.

Suddenly Scuffy knew what had happened to all the water in the well. The mole had burrowed a tunnel through the stream. Instead of filling up the Little Golden Book Land well, the water was rushing into the large mole hole up ahead.

"May I ask you something?" said Scuffy to the mole.

"Ask away," answered the mole.

"What do you plan to do with all that water?" said Scuffy.

"Nothing," said the mole. "I told you—I'm a
mole. I dig holes. I don't mind if there's water in
the holes I dig."

"Do you think you might be able to dig holes
somewhere else?" Scuffy asked hopefully.

"Why should I?" asked the mole.

Scuffy told the mole that the well in Little Golden Book Land was going dry because of the holes the mole was digging. He explained that Tootle would have to haul water from the river, and then he wouldn't be able to give rides to anybody in Little Golden Book Land anymore.

"You get to ride on a train?" asked the mole.

"Sure. Tootle helps everybody get around Little Golden Book Land," said Scuffy. "If you come with me, I'm sure he'll give you a ride."

"I'd love a ride," said the mole.

And what a ride it was! Tootle zigged and zagged around the countryside. Then he chugged up the highest hills and sped down into the deepest valleys. It was a great time for everyone. All the friends had come along to share this special ride with the mole.

At the end, the group of laughing, giggling merrymakers got off the train arm in arm and the mole announced, "I've decided to stop digging my holes in your well. I'm going to start a brand-new tunnel in the Homeway Hollow fields, so I can visit with all my new friends."

"Now our well won't go dry," said Tootle, "and we have Scuffy to thank for that."

"Three cheers for Scuffy," shouted Tawny Scrawny Lion. "Not only did he discover what happened to our well, but he also brought us our new friend, the mole."

"Thanks," said Scuffy, who felt like the biggest and bravest tugboat in the land.